DAY at the BEACH

written and illustrated by
TOM BOOTH

ALADDIN JETER CHILDREN'S

New York   London   Toronto   Sydney   New Delhi

ALADDIN JETER CHILDREN'S

An imprint of Simon & Schuster Children's Publishing Division • 1230 Avenue of the Americas, New York, New York 10020 • First Aladdin hardcover edition May 2018 • Copyright © 2018 by Tom Booth • All rights reserved, including the right of reproduction in whole or in part in any form. • ALADDIN and related logo are registered trademarks of Simon & Schuster, Inc. • For information about special discounts for bulk purchases, please contact Simon & Schuster Special Sales at 1-866-506-1949 or business@simonandschuster.com. • The Simon & Schuster Speakers Bureau can bring authors to your live event. For more information or to book an event contact the Simon & Schuster Speakers Bureau at 1-866-248-3049 or visit our website at www.simonspeakers.com. • Jacket designed by Laura Lyn DiSiena and Tom Booth • Interior designed by Laura Lyn DiSiena • The illustrations for this book were rendered digitally. • The text of this book was set in Burbank. • Manufactured in China 0318 SCP • 10 9 8 7 6 5 4 3 2 1 • Library of Congress Control Number 2017955449 • ISBN 978-1-5344-1105-0 (hc) • ISBN 978-1-5344-1106-7 (eBook)

For my family

One sunny morning on a quiet, sandy beach, as sleepy seagulls swooped and swayed to the soothing sound of the waves . . .

LOOK OUT!

MAKE WAY!

Gideon and his sister, Audrey, raced toward the ocean.

Every summer Gideon and Audrey would build a sand castle.

Together.

Gideon made sure each tower stood straight, every wall was level, and all the castle sides were smooth. Audrey made sure the castle sparkled with shells, sea glass, and a starfish on the top.

But this summer Gideon had a different plan.
He was going to build the most stupendous sand
castle the beach had ever seen.

Alone.

All by himself.

No Audrey.

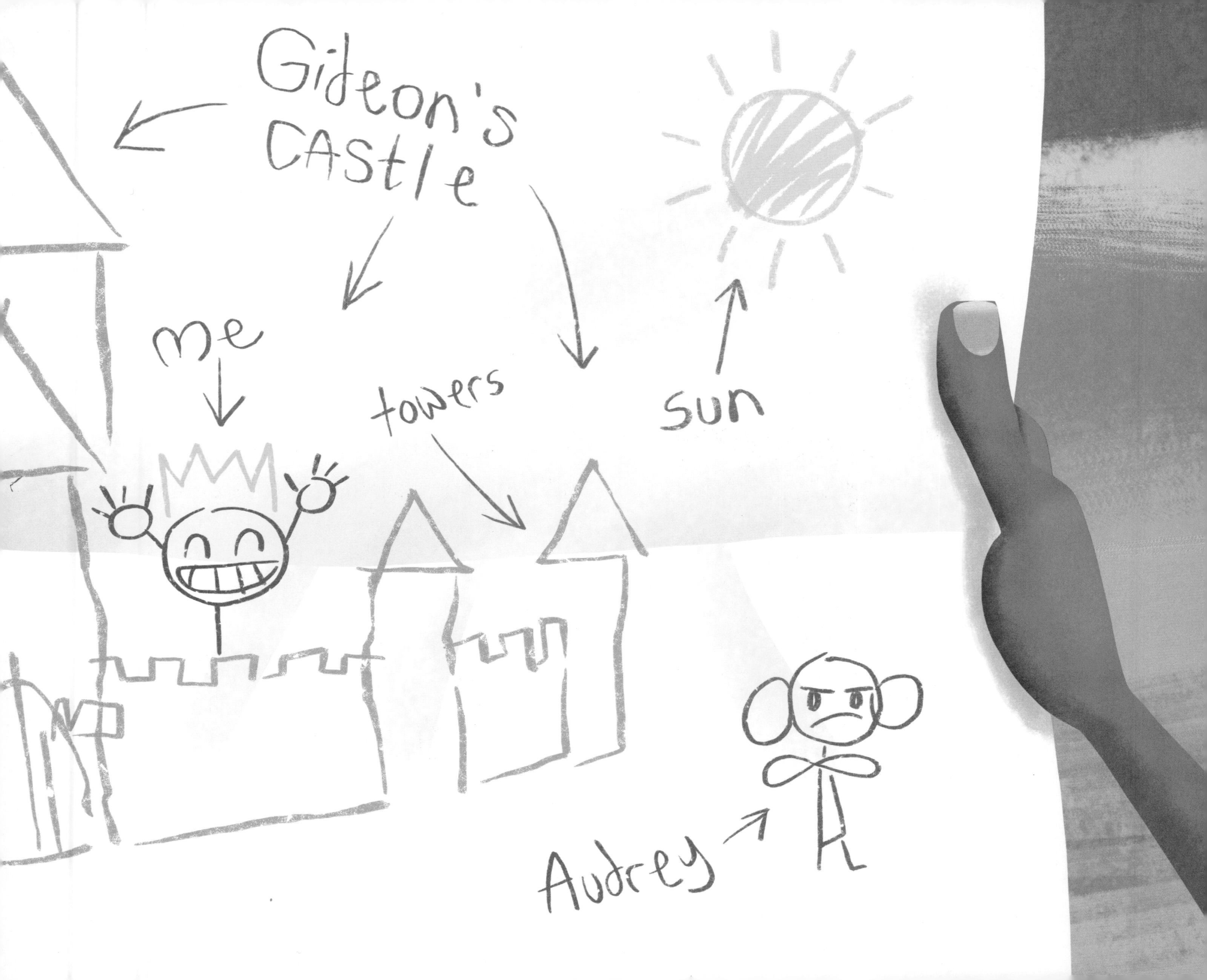
Gideon's CAStle
me
towers
sun
Audrey

"Sand castles are serious business," he told his sister. "Go play with Mom and Dad. The new king of the beach has work to do."

Audrey marched off. . . .

Gideon started digging, shoveling, burrowing, tunneling, piling, and scooping.

He made sure each tower stood straight and every wall was level, and just as he smoothed out the sides of the castle—

"That was just a practice castle," Gideon replied.
He picked up his tools, walked farther down the
beach, and started all over again.

Gideon made sure each tower stood straight and every wall was level, and just when he smoothed out the sides of the castle–

His second castle didn't last much longer than his first.

His third castle would have been perfect, but it was swept away with the tide.

His fourth castle would have won awards, but it shrank beneath a passing shower.

And his sixth castle?

WOOF!

His fifth castle was almost legendary, but it flew away with a strong breeze.

THAT'S IT!

Gideon's patience had run out.
He grabbed his bucket and shovel,
then set out to look for a new spot,
where nothing and no one could
interrupt him.

And finally he found one.
"Perfect!" Gideon said.

He quickly got to work.

Gideon built and he built and he built.
And then he built some more. He made
sure each tower stood straight and
every wall was level, and . . .

As he smoothed out the sides of the castle, everyone on the beach started to walk over.

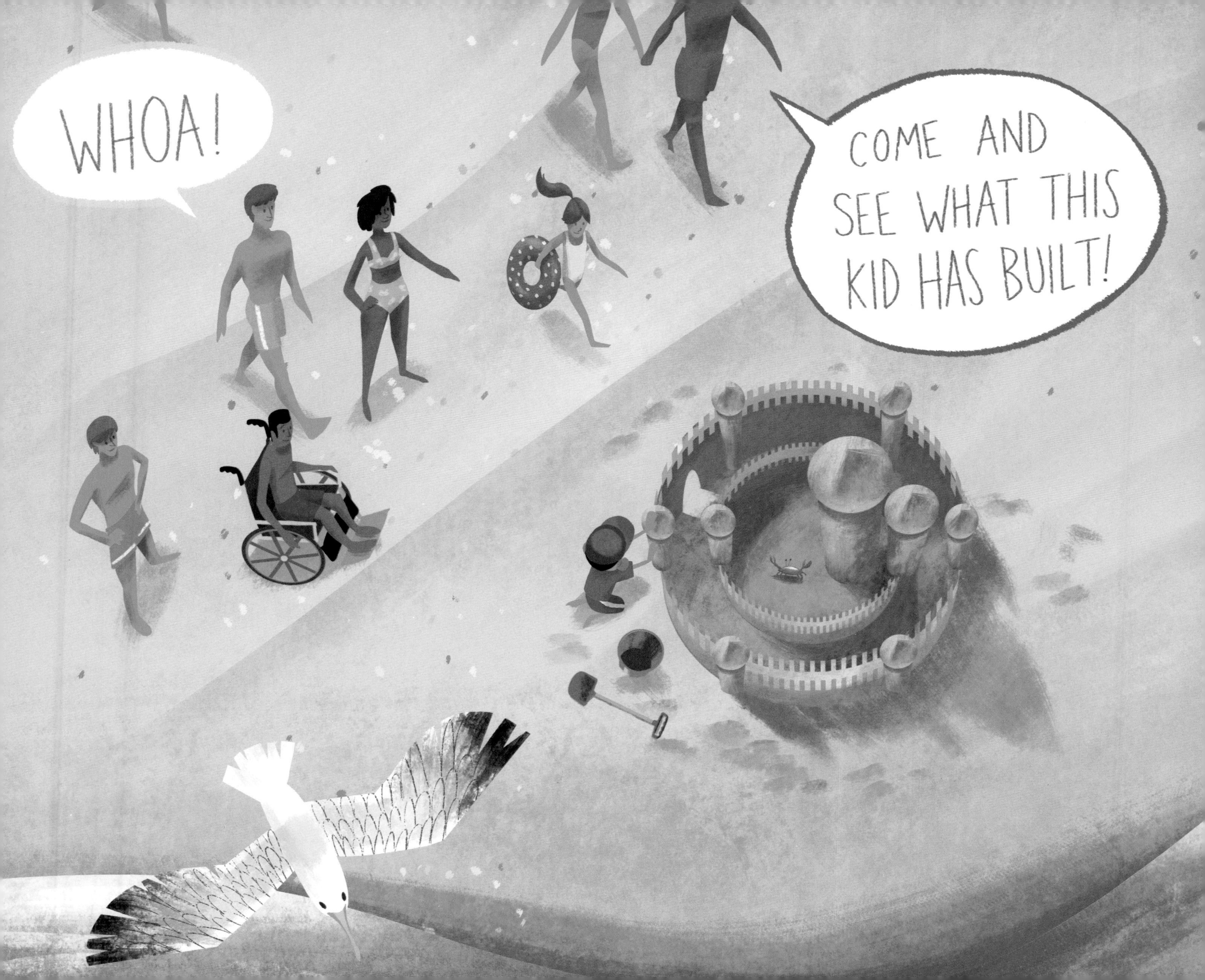
WHOA!
COME AND SEE WHAT THIS KID HAS BUILT!

Gideon loved the crowd's chants and cheers, but then . . .

He spotted Audrey . . .
building a sand castle . . .
with their mom and dad.
And suddenly Gideon was feeling very lonely.

He jumped down and walked across the beach.
Audrey's castle didn't have straight towers, level
walls, or smooth sides.

But it did look like fun.

Gideon glanced over his shoulder at his castle.
Then he looked at Audrey's.
"Room for one more?" he asked.

Audrey grabbed the bucket from her big brother.

"On one condition . . . ," she said with a grin.

"We finish building it . . ."

"Together."